PATRicK

written and illustrated by

QUENTIN BLAKE

CARNIVAL

This edition published in 2000 by Diamond Books
77-85 Fulham Palace Road
Hammersmith, London, W68JB

First published 1968
Reissued 1990
© Quentin Blake 1968
Jonathan Cape Ltd, 20 Vauxhall Bridge Road, London SW1V 2SA

ISBN: 0 00 761008 4
Printed and bound in Italy

This is a story about a young man called Patrick, who set out from his house one day to buy a violin.

In the town the streets were full of stalls. One sold
vegetables, one sold fish and another sold clothes.

These stalls were very interesting but Patrick did not stop until he came to the one kept by Mr Onions. On his stall he had a broken jug, an old lamp, a mouse-trap and all sorts of things that people did not want any more.

"Have you a violin to sell?" asked Patrick.

"You're in luck," said Mr Onions, "I have just one."

Patrick bought the violin with his only silver piece.

He was so pleased that he ran as fast as
he could out into the fields.

When he got there he blew the dust off his violin.

Then he sat down by a pond and began to play a tune. As he played, the most extraordinary thing happened. One by one the fish in the pond began to jump out and fly about in the air. And what is more, they were all different colours and they were singing to the music.

Just then a girl and a boy came along the road.
Their names were Kath and Mick.

"Did you do that?" asked Mick, pointing to the fish
in the air. And Patrick said, "Yes."

Then he played another tune, and the string tying Kath's hair turned into red ribbons and the laces in Mick's boots turned into blue ribbons.

And so the three went down the road together.
Soon they came to an orchard of apple trees. Patrick
played his violin and the leaves on the trees changed
to all kinds of bright colours.

Instead of apples the trees began to grow pears and bananas and cakes and ice-creams and slices of hot buttered toast. Kath and Mick ran about among the trees and helped themselves to whatever they liked.

As they were eating, a flock of pigeons flew down
and Patrick played his violin again. The birds began
to sprout bright new feathers until they were the most
beautiful birds you have ever seen. Kath and Mick
fed them on crumbs of chocolate cake.

After Patrick and the children had gone a little farther, they met some cows. They were white with black spots, but when Patrick played his violin the cows became covered with coloured stars and started to dance to the music.

So they all went along the road together, until they met a tramp. The tramp had whiskers and a hat with a broken top where his hair poked through. He was smoking a pipe and every time he gave a puff sparks flew out of it.

"That's a lovely tune you're playing," said the tramp. "There's nothing I like better than a tune on the violin." So Patrick played even harder, and the sparks from the pipe of the whiskery tramp got bigger and brighter until they were showers of fireworks.

On they all went along the road. It was just like a
procession – Kath and Mick with their ribbons; the
fish and the birds singing; the cows dancing; the
whiskery tramp puffing fireworks from his pipe; and
Patrick playing on his violin.

Before long they met a tinker and his wife with a horse and cart.

"Look at our procession," shouted Kath. "Isn't it fun!"

"How can *he* enjoy it?" asked the tinker's wife. "He's very thin and I don't know what to do for him. He's got a cough and a cold and a stomach-ache and a headache. We have to travel so slowly, I don't know how we shall get to the town before dark."

"Let me play my violin and see what happens," said Patrick.

So he played a tune, and you can see what happened.

The tinker started to get fatter.

He lost his cough, and his cold, and his stomach-ache, and his headache; until he was well and smiling and happy again.

And not only that. Look what happened to his horse and cart! The tinker and his wife climbed on, and so did Patrick and Kath and Mick and the whiskery tramp. The fish and the birds flew above them and the cows galloped along behind.

And they all got back to the town before dark.